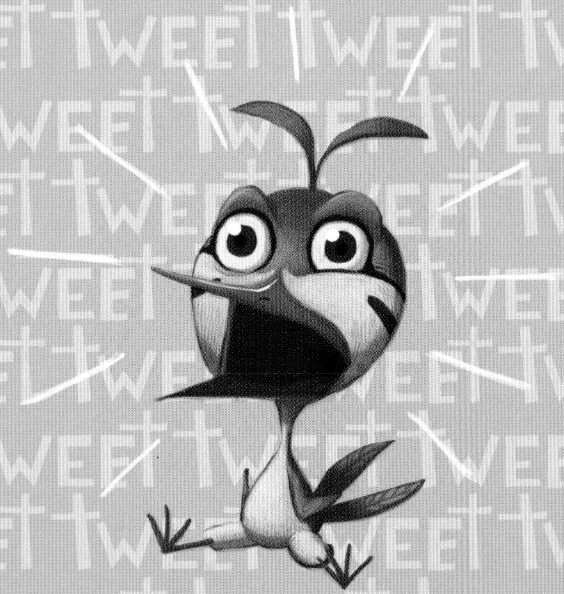

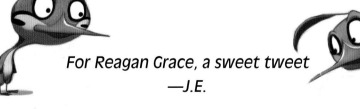

For Reagan Grace, a sweet tweet
—J.E.

For my two tweets, Alek and Kyle
—D.S.

TOM'S TWEET

WRITTEN BY
JILL ESBAUM

ILLUSTRATED BY
DAN SANTAT

Alfred A. Knopf  New York

While hunting one morning, right after a storm,
Tom heard an inquisitive "Tweet?"
And there, to his left,
in the rain-dewy grass,
was a flip-flapping, fluttery . . .
treat!

Tom feasted his eyes on the quivering tot.
"Hello, breakfast," he said with a grin.
He opened his chompers to gobble it down, but . . .
the thing was so wretchedly thin.

"Dadburn it!" said Tom. "You're too skinny to eat.
Why, you're nothing but feather and bone."
He started to leave . . .
but the shivering tweet
looked so frightened.
Unhappy.
Alone.

"I will *not* take you back to your nest," Tom declared.
But the thing blink-blink-blinked, and . . . egad!
Tom was half up the tree with the poor little tyke
when its mama showed up . . .
fighting mad!

Tom mumbled and mumphed, but he couldn't explain
with the tweet in his kisser like that.
Mama Tweet didn't care; she was too busy pecking
(and anyway, birds don't speak Cat).

Tom ran with the tweet
through the garden and yard
in an awkward, undignified crouch.
He scooted past peonies,
pansies, petunias,
and squee-e-e-e-eezed through the rosebushes (*ouch!*).

The baby tweet's black button eyes blink-blink-blinked as it swayed on its wee little feet.
"Consarn it," Tom grumbled. "Now what do I do? Just my luck to get stuck with a tweet."

"Tweet!" chirped the baby.

"Tweet-Tweet!"
"Tweet-Tweet!"
"Tweet-Tweet!"

Tom scowled at the feathery pest.
What was wrong with the thing?
What on earth did it want?
"Will you quit if I build you a nest?"

Tom braved Mama Tweet for a bundle of twigs.
She dive-bombed his noggin.
"Ow! Ow!"

He dropped the tweet onto the twigs and commanded,
"Stop tweeting. Be happy. Right now."

The tot settled into the nest,
but its cries didn't stop.
And why *would* they? Unless . . .
"Dagnabbit," Tom muttered. "There's no way around it.
I'll just have to feed you, I guess."

Tom scritch-scratched and dug
in the storm-puddled mud
for the juiciest worms he could find.
But the tweet wouldn't eat; it was waiting for . . . something.
Tom gasped, "Are you out of your mind?"

With his innards in knots, he selected a wiggler
and gingerly
chewed
it
to
pulp.
He passed the mashed worm
from his mouth
to the baby,
who swallowed it gobbledy-gulp!

Happy at last,
the tweet hopped up on Tom
and explored him,
above
and beneath.
It tugged on his whiskers
and pick-pecked his ears
as he gritted his (still-wormy) teeth.

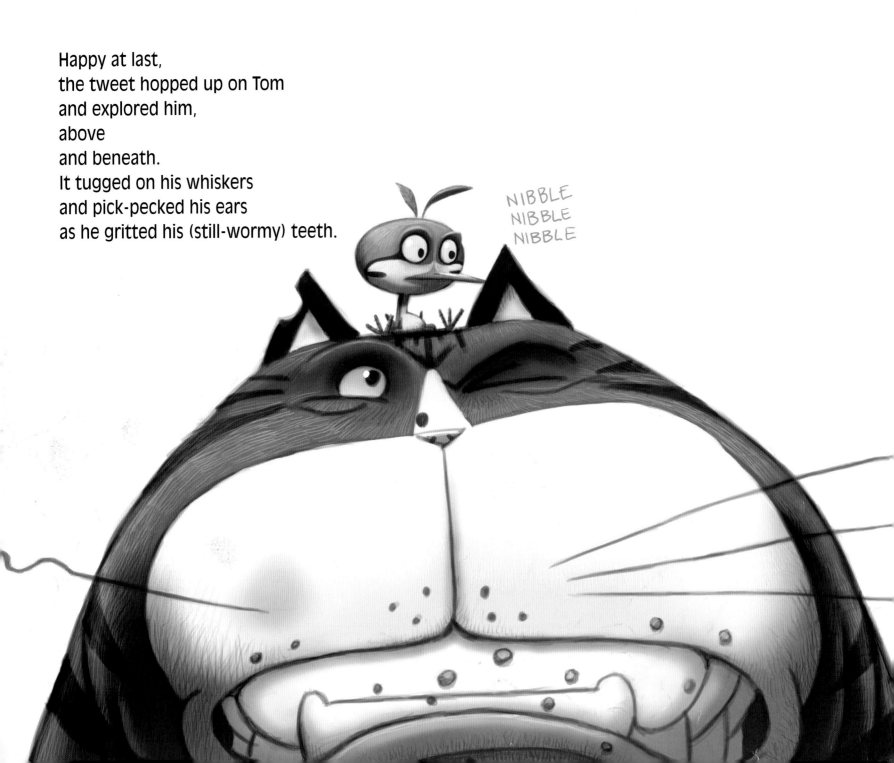

When the little tweet yawned
and hopped under Tom's armpit,
he squirmed away, shaking his head.
"No snuggling," he grumped. "I'm not that kind of cat."
But the wee thing ignored what he said.

Tom sat through the long afternoon
with that tweet wedged in tight
like an unwanted burr.
And although he resisted with all of his might,
from deep down in his chest came a . . .
purrrrr.

Finally, *finally*,
Mama flew off
to find food for the rest of her tots.
"Now's our chance," murmured Tom
to his wakening guest,
sneaking peeks between marigold pots.

"Here you go, little fella," he said. "Home at last.
Say hello to your sister and brothers."
Its feathers atremble, the tweet sadly blinked,
first at Tom,
then the petrified others.

That night, as he slumbered,
Tom dreamed of the tweet?
Was he nuts? How completely absurd!
Yes, as hard as it was for a cat to admit,
he was *missing* that bothersome bird.

Next morning, when Tom stepped from under the porch,
a quick *hop-flutter-plop* caught his eye.
As he rushed to the tree,
he thought, *Nah, couldn't be*.
But it was. It was *his* tweet.
Oh, my.

"Tarnation! You have to stay up there," he said. "You can*not* be my friend. I'm a *cat*!"

But the baby just smiled,
and Tom saw that *this* tweet
didn't care about details like that.

When Mama Tweet saw that old Tom was a softie,
her "sorry" was long (and earsplitting).
And to prove that she trusted him,
really and truly,
she gave him a job . . .

tweety-sitting.

THIS IS A BORZOI BOOK PUBLISHED BY ALFRED A. KNOPF

Text copyright © 2011 by Jill Esbaum
Illustrations copyright © 2011 by Dan Santat

Visit us on the Web! www.randomhouse.com/kids

Educators and librarians, for a variety of teaching tools, visit us at www.randomhouse.com/teachers

Library of Congress Cataloging-in-Publication Data
Esbaum, Jill.
Tom's tweet / by Jill Esbaum ; illustrated by Dan Santat. — 1st ed.
p. cm.
Summary: When a cat finds a bedraggled baby bird that has fallen from its nest, an unlikely friendship develops between the two.
ISBN 978-0-375-85171-1 (trade) — ISBN 978-0-375-95171-8 (lib. bdg.)
[1. Birds—Fiction. 2. Animals—Infancy—Fiction. 3. Cats—Fiction.] I. Santat, Dan, ill. II. Title.
PZ7.E74458Tp 2010
[E]—dc22
2009017262

The illustrations in this book were created using Photoshop. No cats or tweets were mistweeted in the making of this book.

MANUFACTURED IN CHINA

November 2011
10 9 8 7 6 5 4 3 2 1

First Edition

Random House Children's Books supports the First Amendment and celebrates the right to read.